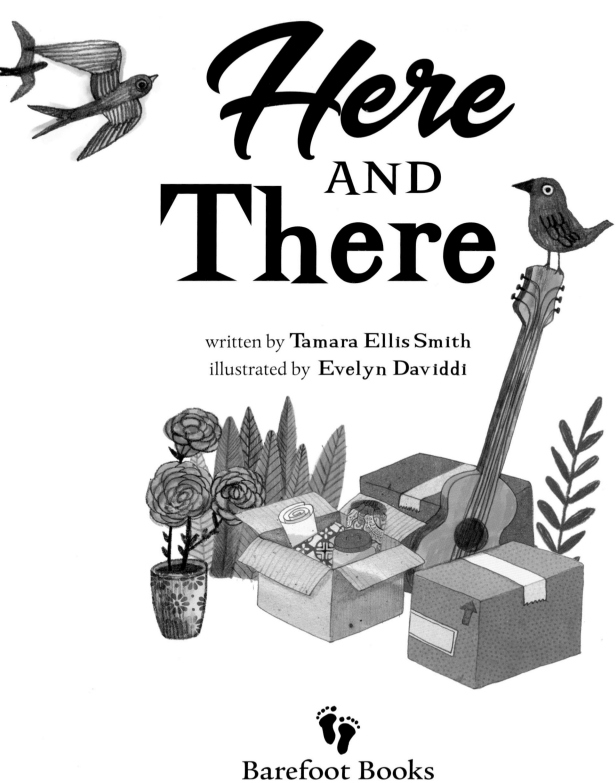

Here
AND
There

written by **Tamara Ellis Smith**

illustrated by **Evelyn Daviddi**

Barefoot Books
Step inside a story

Like the birds he loved,
Ivan rarely kept quiet.

Instead of sitting still,
he crawled through the window,
perched in the pear tree,
stuffed his hands in his pockets
and scattered birdseed.

He drummed like a woodpecker,
cawed like a crow and shrieked like a falcon.

"I'm here! I'm here! I'm here!" Ivan would sing.

Ivan wanted to stay **Here**
(his mama's house),
but he had to go **There**
(his dad's new house).

When he got **There**,
Ivan didn't crawl or perch or stuff or scatter.

"Want me to push you?" asked Dad,
showing him the swing outside.

Ivan folded his arms like wings.

"Where'd you learn to stay so still?" Dad asked.

There, thought Ivan.

(Even when he was sitting right here at his dad's
new house, he thought of it as **There**.)

While he was **There**,
Ivan didn't drum or caw or shriek.

"Want to play robots with me?"
asked Dad, showing him a box filled
with jars, cans and rolls of cloth.

Ivan squeezed his lips into
a sharp beak.

"Where'd you learn
to be so quiet?" Dad asked.

There, thought Ivan again.

Ivan roosted all by himself
around the house,
up in **There**,
around the corner **There**,
and out the door **There**
and **There** and **There**.

He heard a falcon shriek,
but he didn't shriek back.

Then he heard another sound.

Dad was sitting on the porch
with his guitar, strumming a song,
then another, and another,
the way he used to do
when he was **Here**
instead of **There**.

And though Ivan tried
to fold his wings against it,
one song pulled
on his hands
and tugged
at both his feet.

Ivan couldn't be still.

He unfolded his wings,
tapped his toes and
rapped his fingers
on his knees.

He felt the way he did
when Mama lifted him high
to pick pears from the branches
of their tree.

He moved
the way he did
when Dad pushed
him on a swing
as high as the sun.

"I like that," said Ivan,
unsqueezing his lips.
"Where'd you learn to make up songs?"

"I started the tune before I moved," said Dad,
"and I've been working on it more at this house."

"Does the song have words?" asked Ivan.

Dad shrugged his shoulders. "Not yet. Maybe check your pockets?"

So Ivan put his hands in his pockets and found the last bits of birdseed.

Dad played the song again.

Ivan couldn't be quiet.

He drummed, then cawed,
then shrieked, soft
but soon loud, one word,
then two words, then three —

Dad clapped his hands.

"Again!" said Ivan.

Caw Caw!
      Per-chik-o-ree!
Shriek Shriek Drum.
      Feebee Feebee!

Cheer-up. Cheer-up.
      Cheer Cheer Cheer!
Tika-swee. Tika-swee.
      Here Here Here!

Hip-hip-hurrah.
      Zay-zoo-zee-zare.
Peet-zuh. Peet-zuh.
      There There There!

"Where'd *you* learn to make
up songs?" asked Dad.

"Some of it I learned **There**,"
said Ivan, "and some of it **Here**."

Ivan sang and swung and beeped and swooped all weekend until it was time to go back to Mama's house.

He kissed Dad goodbye and said, "I'll be back again soon."

Ivan was glad to see Mama,
but he missed Dad,
and he missed the song
they made together.

Ivan perched
in the pear tree.
He put his hands
in his pockets —

— and found nothing.

"You're so still," said Mama.
"And so quiet."

"I think I lost something,"
said Ivan.

Then he heard a falcon shriek.

"It was **There**," said Ivan.
"And now it's **Here**!"

Ivan checked his pockets again.
He couldn't find the birdseed,
but his fingers found the beat.
Ivan knocked his knees, shrieked to the sky
and flapped his arms like wings.

He had not lost it!
It was **Here**, with him!

Mama heard it too!
She caught the spark
and clapped her hands.
Her feet began to dance.

Ivan took a breath,
and like a bird,
sang his song out loud.

Bird Calls

Caw Caw	American Crow
Per-chik-o-ree	American Goldfinch
Shriek Shriek	Falcon
Drum	Red-bellied Woodpecker
Feebee Feebee	Eastern Phoebe
Cheer-up, Cheer-up	American Robin
Cheer Cheer Cheer	Northern Cardinal
Tika-swee, Tika-swee	Tennessee Warbler
Here Here Here	Indigo Bunting
Hip-hip-hurrah	King Rail
Zay-zoo-zee-zare	Black-throated Green Warbler
Peet-zuh, Peet-zuh	Acadian Flycatcher

For Beka who named the notes,
Kaki who built the bridge and
Jordy who sings the song — T. E. S.

To my lovely friend Silvia — E. D.

Barefoot Books
2067 Massachusetts Ave
Cambridge, MA 02140

Barefoot Books
29/30 Fitzroy Square
London, W1T 6LQ

Text copyright © 2019 by Tamara Ellis Smith. Illustrations copyright © 2019 by Evelyn Daviddi
The moral rights of Tamara Ellis Smith and Evelyn Daviddi have been asserted

First published in the United States of America by Barefoot Books, Inc and in Great Britain by Barefoot Books, Ltd in 2019
All rights reserved

Graphic design by Sarah Soldano, Barefoot Books
Edited and art directed by Kate DePalma, Barefoot Books
Reproduction by Bright Arts, Hong Kong. Printed in China on 100% acid-free paper
This book was typeset in Adriatic, Albertina MT and Baksoda
The illustrations were prepared in mixed media (acrylic paints,
pencil and collage) embellished digitally

Hardback ISBN 978-1-78285-741-9
Paperback ISBN 978-1-78285-742-6
E-book ISBN 978-1-78285-758-7

British Cataloguing-in-Publication Data: a catalogue record for this book
is available from the British Library

Library of Congress Cataloging-in-Publication Data
is available upon request

1 3 5 7 9 8 6 4 2

Barefoot Books
step inside a story

At Barefoot Books, we celebrate art and story that opens the hearts and minds of children from all walks of life, focusing on themes that encourage independence of spirit, enthusiasm for learning and respect for the world's diversity. The welfare of our children is dependent on the welfare of the planet, so we source paper from sustainably managed forests and constantly strive to reduce our environmental impact. Playful, beautiful and created to last a lifetime, our products combine the best of the present with the best of the past to educate our children as the caretakers of tomorrow.

www.barefootbooks.com

Tamara Ellis Smith

pretended she was characters from her most beloved books when she was a child, and spent hours and hours in the woods acting out their stories. Now she lives in Vermont where she is a mother to four children and author of her own books, which she fills with characters who love trees like she does.

Evelyn Daviddi

decided at age seven to become an artist, and she has done exactly that. She studied at the Istituto Europeo di Design in Milan, and now teaches creative illustration at Scuola Internazionale di Comics in Reggio Emilia, Italy. Evelyn has illustrated over forty books for children.